Occidental Haiku

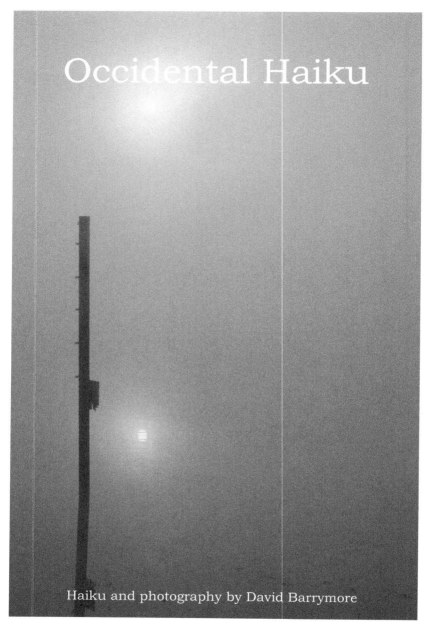

Haiku and photography by David Barrymore

AMZ AMAZON PUBLISHING PROS 2023

Occidental Haiku

Printed in USA

Published through

AMZ AMAZON PUBLISHING PROS

17595 Harvard Ave, Ste C-641,

Irvine, California, 92614

https://amzpublishingpros.com +1-877-992-7638
(USA)

List of Photographs

Preface

Every thunderhead swallowed by cicada, every mountain in a dragonfly's eye, every fleeting world within a drop of dew is Haiku.

Haiku, the ancient, three-line, seventeen syllable, Japanese verse, intimates the interpenetration of life with its surroundings.

Imbued with a western bent at odds with tradition, and a tyro skill that outs its poetaster's pen, these Haiku, my own, are nevertheless heartfelt attempts.

David Barrymore

Thunderhead

Traditional Japanese 5-7-5 meter...

Autumn fireworks!
boots crunch brittle paper shells
crisp air tinged with smoke

Through the veil of rain
through dogwood's lush pink blossoms—
cardinals kissing

Valentine mélange
empty elevator dreams
roses... chocolates...

Temperamental wind—
stalks silent through lush grasses
— scatters brittle leaves

Brilliant head of flame
embers scattered to the stars--
snuffed by winter wind

Under the Bodhi--
lulled to dream, a falling limb
cracks me on the crown

Deep in darkest cave
cold and deadly lizard sleeps
coiled in a skull

Cold out there! He howls...
letting all of winter in
— the door wide open

Where once stood forests...
a flower in a window
in need of water

Burlap gopher sprints...
absquatulates potatoes
sack race champion!

Sun to somber rain
parade yields to procession
colors washed to grey

Misty purple dawn...
wait till sunrise lifts the veil
kiss the face of Fall

Snow falls from a bough
a walker and a jogger
sun crawls up my neck

Curled on grandma's couch
memories of orange warmth...
crack and pop of coal

Balanced on slick stones
spiteful child pisses in
the family well

On a rusted fence
cold and hungry Crow bewails
garden choked with weeds

Shed my leather skin...
lazy in Fall's waning warmth
belly to the sun

Last year I broke ice
this year reading on the porch
—Nature's many moods

Cold lead cloud hangs low...
Crow perched lonely on a wire
—have your friends gone too?

Lost in the torrent...
kind Grandfather tree provides
shelter from the storm

Golden buttercups
and long tall grasses gather
at the old wood shed

Ripples on the lake
booming voice of Thunderhead...
chill upon my skin

Oh! How magnificent
diamond dust upon the lawn
—dewy morning grass

Scarecrow torn from post...
sound of crunching stalks of corn
creeping up my spine

Blue and orange sky
crisp air smells of cedar flame
tree-line silhouette

Do you remember
when you and I were crickets
on a stalk of wheat?

Steamy teapot toots
radiator steams the pane
steamy bowl of soup

Hunger sniffs my hand---
garden-fresh potatoes peeled
almost oven-ripe!

Oh! Cruel bedbugs
to breakfast, lunch, and dinner
on a starving man!

Brava! I applaud
your death scene Ms. Mosquito
—Oh! and real blood too!

Sac of dung laid out
thorns and weeds grow from his grave
—rumors of a snake!

Muddy *Welcome* mat
and puddles where friends shake rain
from their umbrellas

By tread of their shoes
Mother knows who tracked the mud
on her kitchen floor

Brushstrokes green and blue
beginnings of a mountain
—early morning mist

Flowers bow with rain
briars wreath a rusted swing
toad chants solemn tones

At my funeral
friends discuss the smooth red wheels
of an apple cart

Shores of chocolate sand...
an island sinks into a
sea of steaming milk

White cat sleeps content
on a rug upon the vent
—snow blankets the lawn

Cicada

Haiku as three-line free verse...

Snowflake kisses
tender on the neck
belie cold iron gate

Mist dissipates...
starlight
cool and clear

Sweating... sweating...
even the glass of ice water
sweating... sweating...

Christmas cookies...
the spatula
a microphone

Tender shoot
cracks the concrete
to nibble sun

Slug and I
lag behind
—Fall twilight

So many stars!
I should have brought
more marshmallows

Warms one
with its steady flame
--Solitude

Mother chose
the perfect shade of green
to carpet forest floor

Spelunk!
right before my eyes...
a spider!

Tragedy...
King Frost lopped
Daffodil's head

Storm blew through...
now purple dogwood petals
dust the street

Stop squirming, Fly
I'm trying to free you
from the web

Frost's cruel fingers
pluck pink petals
from my dogwood

Sunlight's
kiss
breaks the ice

Now the autumn leaves
have gone...
dingy cracked facades

Howling wind...
a chill runs through
the empty house

Ocean
deep with wonder
forgets itself

Walking through the field...
briars
tag along

Falling leaves
sinking Autumn sun...
Soon come drifts of down

Fierce winds...
Jonquils loose their
yellow hats

Cardinal shakes the snow
that fell from
Squirrel's leap

A cold man?
Yes...
I wear coat he gave me

Windy day!
Grey Stone holds the door
for Muddy Boots

Down the street
a man planting flowers
Sneezing

O.K.
Ant...
you win

Downstream
leaf and branch
part ways

Forest deep—
cracking of a
bony limb

Lonely meal...
Moonlight takes her place
beside me

Mercury
moon and earth
frozen in place

Cat's paw
a
sun visor

Wherever
cats sleep
sunlight finds them

Old Turtle
drinks the coolness of
a moonlit stream

All at once...
the tree sprouts
hungry birds

Trundling up
the mountain
-- the moon-face monk

Hours!
and yet that drop of rain...
still hanging on

Morning fog...
a white cat prowls
the riverbank

Cat's paw
wet with
grasses' dew

On my bed
of wilted flowers...
old black Crow

37

Smiling...
cozy in her
cat bed

In the ivy patch...
a fluffy brown tail
searches for its squirrel

Breathe Death
and soon
the flies, the maggots!

On a nameless headstone
overrun with moss and weeds...
a butterfly

A
spire
in mist

Weeping Willows
gather by the stream
to drink

A grey cloud
A grey cat
crossing the street

Cool loam
of a privy hedge...
sleepy-eyed rabbit

Stone church...
above the arch
a sleeping bat

Shadow of his flag
sours my
apple tree

Bed of rock
smoothed by cool and
patient stream

Briars thick—
I should find
another path

Barren tree...
with Cardinals
apple-fat

Cicada—
it shell hangs from a tree
—ascends with wings

Screaming wind rattles the gate
... and...
lifts the latch?

Above the
air conditioning...
droning of cicada

Autumn dusk...
loneliness and shadows
drawing near

Just before they meet
two fireflies
wink out

Last parking spot...
ankle-deep
in rain water

Click beetle
scurries up the
bamboo stalk

Cooling on the ledge...
sunbaked loaf
of calico

So near...
the wind from
horsefly's wing

The rain...
the ticking of the clock...
the drum of fingers...

My tired blood...
mosquitoes
easier to swat

Firefly...
running...
down...

Yawning wide
a gnat
flew in my mouth

Passing clouds ...
faces of old friends
long gone

Chasing down an old friend
I won
second place!

Can't sleep
for Cricket's
snoring

I've walked this path before...
old tracks
still in the mud

Rising breath
behind the snowdrift...
I see you!

Littered field...
empty shopping carts
at the bus stop

Brick facade
warm with
forenoon sun

New year's day
alone
not vomiting

Plastic bag
in an empty lot
plays Jellyfish

Cloudy night...
yellow eye
of a black cat—

Playful fish...
the stream
giggling

After rain...
all is fresh
and new again

Each spring
tall white flowers
meeting at the fence

Spring morning
fresh mown clumps of humid grass
earthy smell of cows

Chipmunk—
just what he can stuff
in his cheeks

Splash!
flash of silver scales
across the moonlit lake

Angry child...
trampling the rose
that was his mother

Pink dogwood
plucks a cardinal
from the sky

Maple tree caught
a leaping squirrel...
yellow leaves cascade

They suck and suck
it's never enough
—bloody mosquitoes!

Yellow leaf
coming down to lay
beside me

Sun shines down
on a honeybee bathing
in rose water

Parking...
acorns
crunching

Woodwind, flute
and golden horn
—sunrise symphony

Without warning...
chill snuffs
candle's flame

Christmas card
I promised uncle...
bookmark in a dusty tome

For the turtle...
breaking to
a stop

Field so thick with crickets
I could walk to the moon
on their voices!

At the red light
a fly through one window
out the other

Cardinal
so regal with his mitre
and robes of red

Night
night,
Cricket

Dragonfly

Haiku as couplet...

Sultry smoky summer night
Drunken moths swarm neon light.

Dreaming lush and fragrant bloom
Boots crunch icy Winter gloom.

Humid haze of gripping heat--
Dog slips from its master's leash.

Tired heavy limbs at length
Oak, I beg an ounce of strength!

Look! Nandina berries red
Look again! A cardinal's head.

Every prickly blade of grass
Tickles tiny toes that pass.

Even with a thousand eyes
Spider's web traps hapless flies.

Autumn's liquid sunset pools
Red and gold as evening cools.

Winter wind whips talon black
Pushes Crow; Crow pushes back.

Scenic trail retrievers guide
Their master too preoccupied.

Sunshine melts the icy cold
Potholes puddle liquid gold.

Deathly pale the winter sun
Sky of white and earth all one.

Sugar maple honey brown
Drizzles Autumn on the town.

Sticky rain-slick city sleeps
Hush the rush of busy streets.

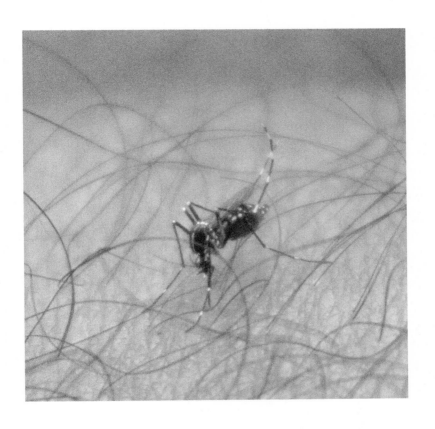

Fickle grey March day
Will it snow? Will it rain?

Cotton flurry soft and fleet
Spans the meadow in a leap.

Grumble rumble round the tree
Not a raindrop falls on me.

Hammock days of lazy heat
Yawning limbs stretch, moan, and creak.

Upon my knee, the wise old cat
When I died, stone Buddha's lap.

Cold through holes in Winter clothes
Nips arms and fingers, feet and toes.

Dan DeLion asks to dance
Shrinking Violet takes a chance.

Ha! Ha! At last, the full moon free
Disentangled from the tree.

Vines cling as I walk away
I too, friends, would rather stay.

Cotton sweater fuzzy tight
Morning warm from laundry night.

We hook our fur and leather hide
To roast our flesh by fireside.

Dew

Haiku as tercet...

Pacer leads the pack
'round and 'round and 'round and 'round
'round the greyhound track

Bluebird quite the sight!
chestnut breast a dapper vest
trousers cotton white

Autumn night
bright enough to write
by moonlight

More than one could ask--
starlight pours itself inside
this tiny human flask

Sweating in my sleep
fever dance of fire ants
— midnight summer heat

Nature's grand design—
flowers bloom among the tombs
fertile earth enshrines

Autumn skies aglow
cool breeze scatters fallen leaves...
fires burning low

Geese parade the streets
gander gawk all traffic stops
honk honk honking beaks

Rumbling of the storm
in my head I'm home in bed...
blankets dry and warm

City lost to mist
creeping down the sleepy street...
ceases to exist

Carpenter bee
hoovers hoovers hoovers
above me

Golden thread that binds...
unseen weaver of the dream
witnesses divine